PLAY RHYMES

collected and illustrated by

MARC BROWN

COLLINS

The author and publishers haved tried to trace the copyright holders of the music on pages 30-32. In the event of any question arising they will be pleased to make the necessary correction in future editions.

Copyright © 1987 by Marc Brown

First published in Great Britain by
William Collins Sons & Co Ltd 1988
Originally published in the United States by
E. P. Dutton, New York, a division of NAL Penguin, Inc.

British Library Cataloguing in Publication Data

Brown, Marc
  Play rhymes.
  1. Children's finger play rhymes in
  English – Anthologies
  I. Title
  398'.8
  ISBN 0-00-195490-3

Printed and bound in Spain by Cronion S.A.

for our newest playmate,

ELIZA MORGAN BROWN

Contents

John Brown's Baby

 John Brown's baby had a cold upon its chest,

John Brown's baby had a cold upon its chest,

John Brown's baby had a cold upon its chest,

And they rubbed it with camphorated oil.

The Counting Game

 One, two, buckle my shoe;

 Three, four, knock at the door;

 Five, six, pick up sticks;

 Seven, eight, stand up straight;

 Nine, ten, ring Big Ben;

 Eleven, twelve, dig and delve.

Do Your Ears Hang Low?

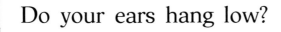 Do your ears hang low?

Do they wobble to and fro?

Can you tie them in a knot?

Can you tie them in a bow?

Can you throw them over your shoulder

Like a continental soldier?

Do your ears hang low?

The Noble Duke of York

Oh, the noble Duke of York,

He had ten thousand men;

He marched them up to the top of the hill,

And he marched them down again.

Now when they were up, they were up;

And when they were down, they were down;

But when they were only halfway up,

They were neither up nor down.

The Crocodile

She sailed away on a happy summer day,

On the back of a crocodile.

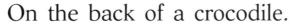
"You'll see," said she,

"he's as tame as tame can be;

I'll ride him down the Nile."

The croc winked his eye

as she bade them all good-bye,

Wearing a happy smile.

At the end of the ride,

the lady was inside,

And the smile on the crocodile.

Teddy Bear

 Teddy Bear, Teddy Bear, turn around.

 Teddy Bear, Teddy Bear, touch the ground.

 Teddy Bear, Teddy Bear, show your shoe.

 Teddy Bear, Teddy Bear, that will do!

 Teddy Bear, Teddy Bear, go upstairs.

 Teddy Bear, Teddy Bear, say your prayers.

 Teddy Bear, Teddy Bear, turn off the light.

 Teddy Bear, Teddy Bear, say good-night.

My Bicycle

One wheel, two wheels, on the ground,

My feet make the pedals go round and round.

Handlebars help me steer so straight,

Down the pathway, through the gate.

Elephant

Right foot, left foot, see me go.

I am grey and big and slow.

I come walking down the street

With my trunk and four big feet.

Bears, Bears, Everywhere

 Bears, bears, everywhere!

 Climbing stairs

 Sitting on chairs

 Collecting fares

 Painting squares

 Bears, bears, everywhere!

Animals

Can you hop like a rabbit?

Can you jump like a frog?

Can you walk like a duck?

Can you run like a dog?

Can you fly like a bird?

Can you swim like a fish?

And be still like a good child—

As still as this?

Wheels on the Bus

 The wheels on the bus go round and round,

Round and round, round and round.

The wheels on the bus go round and round,

All through the town.

 The driver on the bus says, "Move on back,

Move on back, move on back."

The driver on the bus says, "Move on back,"

All through the town.

 The children on the bus say, "Yak yak yak,

Yak yak yak, yak yak yak."

The children on the bus say, "Yak yak yak,"

All through the town.

The mummies on the bus say, "Shh shh shh,
Shh shh shh, shh shh shh."
The mummies on the bus say, "Shh shh shh,"
All through the town.

I'm a Little Teapot

I'm a little teapot, short and stout.

Here is my handle, here is my spout.

When I start to steam up, then I shout,

Tip me over and pour me out.

John Brown's Baby

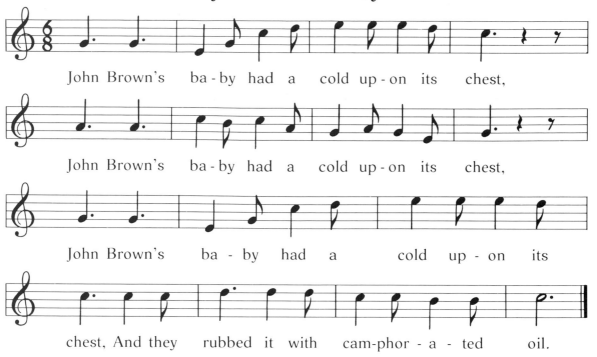

John Brown's ba-by had a cold up-on its chest,

John Brown's ba-by had a cold up-on its chest,

John Brown's ba - by had a cold up - on its

chest, And they rubbed it with cam-phor - a - ted oil.

Do Your Ears Hang Low?

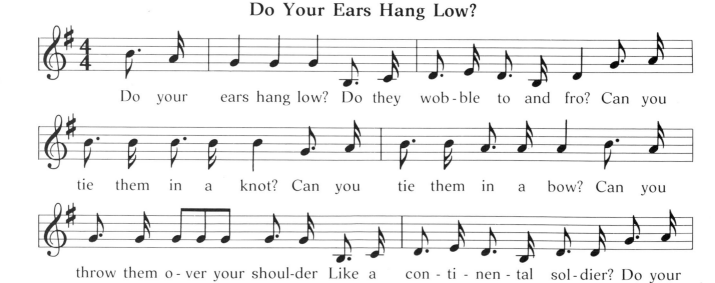

Do your ears hang low? Do they wob-ble to and fro? Can you

tie them in a knot? Can you tie them in a bow? Can you

throw them o-ver your shoul-der Like a con-ti-nen-tal sol-dier? Do your

ears hang low?

The Noble Duke of York

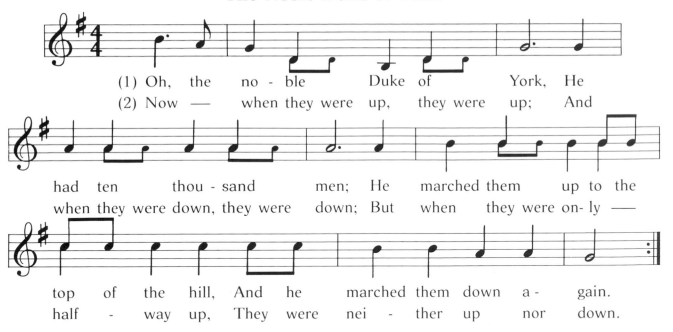

(1) Oh, the no-ble Duke of York, He
(2) Now — when they were up, they were up; And

had ten thou-sand men; He marched them up to the
when they were down, they were down; But when they were on-ly —

top of the hill, And he marched them down a- gain.
half - way up, They were nei - ther up nor down.

The Crocodile

She sailed a-way on a hap-py sum-mer day, On the back of a cro-co-

dile. "You'll see," said she, "he's as tame as tame can be; I'll

ride him down the Nile." The croc winked his eye as she

bade them all good-bye, Wear-ing a hap-py smile. At the

end of the ride, the la-dy was in-side, And the smile on the cro-co- dile.

Wheels on the Bus

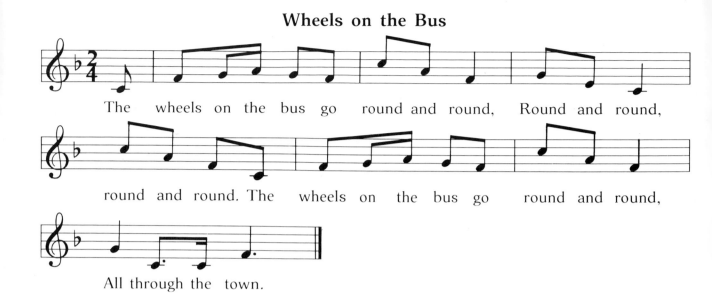

The wheels on the bus go round and round, Round and round,

round and round. The wheels on the bus go round and round,

All through the town.

The driver on the bus says, "Move on back,
Move on back, move on back."
The driver on the bus says, "Move on back,"
All through the town.

The children on the bus say, "Yak yak yak,
Yak yak yak, yak yak yak."
The children on the bus say, "Yak yak yak,"
All through the town.

The mummies on the bus say, "Shh shh shh,
Shh shh shh, shh shh shh."
The mummies on the bus say, "Shh shh shh,"
All through the town.

I'm a Little Teapot

I'm a lit-tle tea-pot, short and stout. Here is my

han-dle, here is my spout. When I start to steam up,

then I shout, Tip me o-ver and pour me out.